Carrot the Parrot

Other Books by Theresa

ROSETEARS:
A Journey of Loving God, Loving Ourselves,
and Loving Others

The Rosetears Discovery Journal:
A Workbook Companion to ROSETEARS

The St. Francis Prayer Discovery Journal:
12 Prayers for Personal Peace

Friday Love Notes for the Soul:
52 Meditations in Just a Few Words and a Little Bit of Art

Carrot the Parrot
and the Island of Letting Go

A Storybook about Love & Letting Go

Written and illustrated by
Theresa Wyatt Prebilsky

Sacred Support
Publishing llc

For my grandmothers,

Dora Dalrymple Rogers and
Florence Cutsinger Wyatt

Contents

*I see so many beautiful horizons,
such infinitely varied tints, that the palette
of the Divine Painter will alone,
after the darkness of this life, be able to supply me
with the colours wherewith I may portray
the wonders that my soul descries.*[1]

– St. Thérèse of Lisieux

[1] Boer, S. P. (1912). The Story of a Soul: The Autobiography of St. Thérèse of Lisieux. London: Burns, Oates, & Washbourne.

Welcome

Welcome to my little world of fun and love with friends.

I first met Carrot the Parrot one Tuesday evening while meditating with a handful of people that I have come to trust and cherish as fellow journeyers. When I opened my eyes that evening and returned my attention back to the room and to where my shoes were, I could barely stay in my seat! I was so surprised and delighted to have met such vivid characters and personalities in my quiet time with God. I was also humbled by the sweet little love story that was laid out before me without me even having to ask.

Since that first meeting, Myra's journey has become, for me, a celebration of finding love and forgiveness with friends on the journey. Now, as I sit here writing to you, I cannot help but wonder if this story is for adults who are awakening or getting re-acquainted with their child within, or for children who are already familiar with the sweet simple joy of being themselves in the now. It is a question that I am willing to leave answered by you, with love.

Love is big, and small.

— *Emanuel (Manu) Raul Fai-Yengo*

CHAPTER 1

Get In The Boat

yra stood on the edge of the sandy shore, facing east and into the early sun rising. She felt the saltwater sting in her eyes and the warm welcoming waves touching and teasing the tips of her shoes.

She knew if she did not stop staring into the infinite horizon and start moving soon, either back up the hill behind her or into the boat loosely tethered to a very weathered dock in front of her, she would sink further into the mud on the edge of things.

Myra knew she had to make a decision.

Lifting the hem of her blue & white checkered cotton dress much higher than necessary, and pulling on her beloved and misshaped hat from her happy days in the meadow, Myra said to herself,

"The sea seems too big—way too big and too deep for me. And this boat is way too small for any kind of a long trip."

She looked for a sign and listened for a hint of encouragement in the rhythm of the waves and the song of the gulls, but having heard none, she considered,

"If I get into the boat without a friend, a map, and something to eat, I might get lost and starve."

Myra started crying really, really hard—like you do when there does not seem to be an easy way up or down, forward or backward. Between her tears and crying-hiccups, she was finally able to find her words to say out loud,

"What if I get lost and no one comes looking for me?"

Myra's tears got fewer and quieter as she wished and waited for an answer, or for someone to show up and sit beside her while she worried.

But, as the day went on, Myra began accepting that no one was going to come for her and help her decide what to do. So, she crouched down on her knees, listened to the quiet voice inside her, turned her face to the rising sun and declared,

"I am afraid, but I know what I have to do. I have to get into that boat."

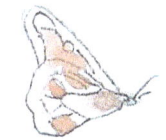

That's when Myra noticed the tingle in her toes and the butterflies in her tummy — familiar signs that she was being given courage to take the next right step even though it felt like the hardest thing to do by herself.

Myra unclenched her hands and dropped the hem of her dress. Turning away from the water, she heard these encouraging words whispered into her ear,

"Get in the boat, Myra. You will not be alone."

At first Myra stepped back in stubborn refusal, but not for awfully long, because she slowly and surely recognized the voice inside as familiar, kind, and speaking truth into her heart.

"I am your friend, Myra," she heard. "I brought along crackers — your favorite kind — and we don't need a map. I know where we are, and I know where we are going."

And that is how Myra got unstuck from the mud and got into the boat.

CHAPTER 2

Stay in the Boat

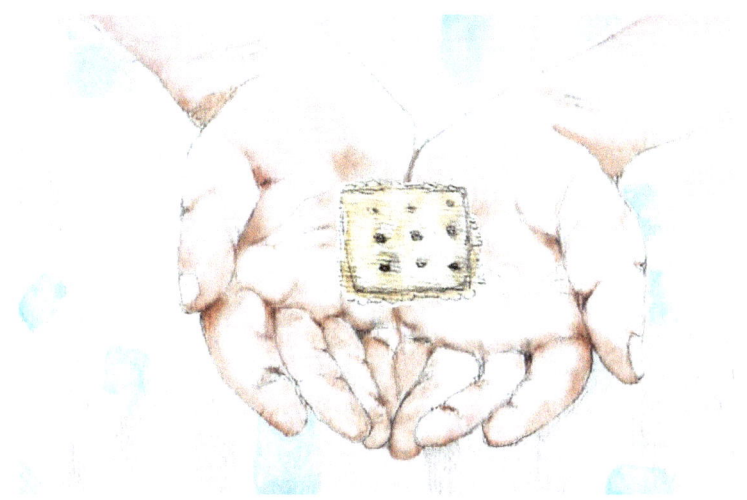

When Myra stepped into the little boat she felt slightly queasy, and surprised! Because she realized that a tall and lanky man was already sitting at the other end.

When he introduced himself as Christopher, Myra accepted his presence with unexpected ease. Then, without a want or a need for further explanations, Christopher casually opened a white tin box of square, scalloped-edged crackers, said a little prayer of plenty, and offered Myra saltines to eat slowly and one at a time.

When he saw that Myra had relaxed and was settling in nicely, Christopher stood up and began steering the small craft away from the shore. Without sounding too big or too small, he calmly said,

"You are doing very well, Myra. Now soften your gaze and keep your eyes on the horizon."

And what do you know?

Before not very long at all, Myra noticed that her tummy was relaxed. Her toes too! Why, she even let herself take a little nap as the boat gently rocked and swayed like a red and white bobber in the sparkling sea of blues.

When Myra woke up, a little bit stiff and achy and still rubbing sleep from her eyes, she noticed in the far, far distance, an island. She groggily asked her companion,

"What is that little speck of land that I see away-far-away? Is that where we are going?"

Myra looked across the water in front of her and all around her. When she turned and looked behind her, she saw the shores of home receding further and further away and became very afraid of the little boat sinking.

Myra panicked!

Myra pulled her hat down a bit tighter and tried to use her best thinking to calm herself. But, as much as she tried, she could not stop the too-many questions flying all around her like curious crows looking for shiny things to collect and carry to somewhere else.

"Where are we going? And why are we going there?" she breathlessly asked. "When will we get there? How long will it take?" she continued.

"Do we have enough food?" she added with increasing alarm. "What if it starts storming with wild winds and rain and loud thunder and blinding lightning? What will we do if that happens?"

Myra gulped another big breath of air and screeched at the top of her lungs, "WHAT IF IT GETS DARK and we get LOST, or TOO MUCH WATER gets into our….."

"E-n-o-u-g-h," Christopher interrupted with more gaiety than Myra thought appropriate or kind. "I do believe," he lightly chuckled, "that you are more afraid of what might scare you later than what is happening right now!"

"Myra," he assured her, "I have known you all of your life, and I know you pretty well."

"I know what makes you giggle and what makes you cry. I know what delights you and frightens you. When you forget who you are, as you sometimes do, that is okay, because I remember just how creative, curious, and courageous you truly are. And, I will always stay with you until you remember this too."

"Stay in the boat," he added. "We are closer to the island than you think. In fact, look! We are here!"

And by gum, when Myra dared to peek through her fingers pressed ever so tightly against her face, she saw the island was but a hop, skip, and a jump away.

CHAPTER 3

Arrival

nd that is exactly what happened next! Myra hopped, skipped, and jumped to the inviting island's shore.

Myra opened her eyes wide and drank in the sights of lovely long landscapes, valleys and grassy streams snaking their lazy way through green pastures and rolling hills gently inviting her to explore. Delighted, she danced on the soft mossy carpets beneath her bare feet.

Myra did not have to think too long or too hard about where to begin her hike to the hills. The inviting path was well marked and flanked with colorful guideposts made of tall yellow sunflowers shouldering blue morning glories.

The way was so easy and delightful, in fact, that she barely noticed how far she had traveled when she reached the top of the highest of hills.

There, Myra stopped.

She put her hands on her hips, took three long, deep breaths of air to slow down her pounding heart and racing mind, then slowly turned to take in the 360-degree view of splendor — up and down and all around her.

Myra knew she had never been there before, but the sights and sounds felt strangely familiar.

"What is this place?" Myra mused. "Why does it feel so much like home even though I KNOW I have never been here before?"

Just as Myra had finished this thought, she noticed a small patch of her favorite flowers, a butterfly bath, and a simple brass plaque inscribed with an invitation to be in this Thin Space.

Welcome Sojourner

This Thin Space has been created by
layers and layers of intentions and prayers
whispered over millions of years.

Here, may you safely and lovingly experience
the new as old—the old as new,
the where as here—and the always now.

May you remember and reclaim
what you hold as precious but may have lost
somewhere along the way.

May you dare to step into
bold reckonings with your past,
and even bolder dreams for your future.

May you deeply know the loss and freedom
of letting go,
and allow yourself to grieve alone
in silent companionship.

This space is made sacred
by all who have come before you,
and by you as you stand in this moment.

May you be blessed
as this land is now blessed by you.

As Myra pondered all of these possibilities, imagine how surprised she was when she turned and saw her grandmothers waiting for her at the top of the hill!

CHAPTER 4

The Grandmothers

Myra had loved her Grandmother Dora, her mother's mother.

She loved the way her grandmother looked in her home-sewed yet fashionable blue dress and yellowing, pinkish-toned string of pearls.

Myra loved the way she smelled — a combination of lilac-perfumed dusting powder and buttered breakfast toast.

She loved how adventurous and independent her grandmother was — like the way her grandmother added ingredients to make recipes her own, traveled alone to new cities, or dared to be happy even when life had been hard for her or for the people around her that she loved so very much.

Standing to Myra's right, with arms akimbo and exuding a city girl's confidence, Grandma Dora looked with great love and confidence upon Myra and said,

"Child, I was with you the day you were born. On that day," she continued, "I recognized your inherent courage to endure hardships without losing your belief in Good and in yourself."

"Remember, my dear Myra, when you get discouraged or afraid, and want to run away from others or from yourself—reclaim the courage to be who you are and how you are made."

"Thank you, Grandmother," Myra replied, "I will remember."

Myra also loved her Grandmother Florence, her father's mother.

She loved sitting with her grandmother in the corner of the yard they had together whimsically named The Limberlost.

Myra was delighted in the soothing sounds she could hear when being with her Grandma Florence — the shy song of a brave bird in spring, the gentle rustle of leaves in autumn, the far-off drone of a tractor turning dirt in the fields, or the nothingness sounds of living in the country.

Sitting peacefully beside her in the grass to her left, Grandmother Florence opened her arms wide with a flare uncharacteristic of her grandmother's country reserve, and said, "Little one, I too was with you on the day you were born."

"From the first few moments of meeting you, I recognized your inherent love and connection with nature."

"From your earliest days, I watched as you made sense of personal chaos by looking deeply into the nature of things around you — the bleeding hearts of spring, the chartreuse green apples of summer, the wobbly woolly worms of autumn, and the moody blue-gray shades of moonlit snow in winter."

"Remember," she urged, "nature is one of your pathways to being and remembering who and what you are. Dig your roots deep into the earth where you are planted, yet always be willing to bend like the willow you knew on the farm."

"Thank you, Grandmother," Myra replied, "I will remember."

Myra marveled at all of the mysteries and wonders that her grandmothers had brought to her that day, then exclaimed,

"WOW, I DO remember the willow!"

"I do remember the eerie blues of winter, the woolly worms, the green apples, and the bleeding hearts."

"I DO remember the courage I have to be who I am when at first, running away and giving up feels oh so much easier."

When Myra turned to thank her grandmothers, she noticed that they were now sitting down, together, with her. She knew they were preparing to tell her more.

CHAPTER 5

The Silver Platter

M yra shifted a bit and planted her feet on the ground as she had been taught, became still as a mouse, and listened intently as the grandmothers spoke with one collective voice.

"Myra, our child, we see the pain in your heart and hear the worry in your mind. What still hides in your heart as hurts?" they asked. "What remains too big to talk about, yet too small a splinter to explain how much it still hurts?"

The grandmothers watched as Myra thought about these things, then with great compassion asked,

"Are you willing to recall and name what hurt you, or scared you, confused or disappointed you when you were littler?"

"Are you willing to recall and name those whom you may have hurt, scared, confused or disappointed?"

Myra tucked her skirt beneath her, sat down on a moss-covered log, and listened with her heart to hear what was indeed stealing her joy.

As thoughts and tears moved from her heart to her throat, Myra intuitively reached for the ragged edged, gray rock that she wore on a necklace beneath her frock. She thoughtfully tumbled the cold stone between her fingers as she remembered the hurts she had caused others.

Then she carefully removed it and placed it on a silver platter sitting before her, and watched as the lusterless rock changed to a smoothly polished, violet-purple amethyst crystal.

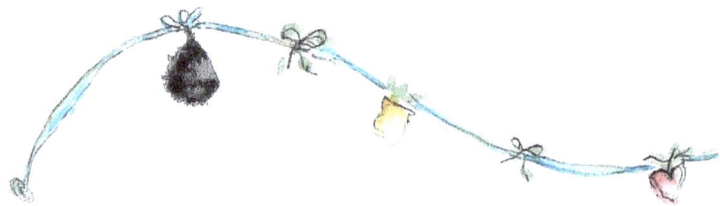

Next, Myra slowly but deliberately reached for a second rock of equal weight strung on her necklace. This rock wore heavy for it held painful memories of being hurt, left out or forgotten. She felt the red-hot heat of re-lived anger in the fiery stone, then removed it and also placed it on the platter.

Myra's tears moved from her throat to her eyes as she watched the red rock change to the splendid shape and sparkle of a small, but finely cut, pink diamond.

With surprising ease and a quiet knowing, Myra continued to remember and release all of her secret disappointments and hurts — placing each and every one of them onto the silver platter sparkling in the sun.

When all thoughts and tears trailed and diminished to a single drop, Myra knew she was finished.

Myra watched as the sun on the platter changed to long shadows of evening and the trees and mountains became black silhouettes against bold golden skies. She instinctively bowed in gratitude and respect for all that had been revealed and withheld, and to the Good she felt present in her mind and in her heart.

Then, with courage to wholly be as she was made, and with nature in and all around her and her grandmothers nearby, Myra laid her head down and slept.

CHAPTER 6

Finding Flight

When Myra woke up, it took her a moment or two to remember all of the mysteries and miracles of the night before, and to notice that the grandmothers and the lovely silver platter were no longer beside her.

Myra felt deeply the familiar sadness of too many goodbyes said in driveways on Sunday afternoons, and too many we'll-stay-in-touch promises made when people moved away.

Where lightness and ease were in her heart the day before, she felt shadier and heavier feelings, and asked, "Why do things have to change? I much prefer the way things were yesterday than feeling this sadness today."

Just as Myra was truly sinking in spirit, she heard a gentle voice meeting her where she was.

"Sadness is natural in the seasons of living and loving."

"When the last tulip of spring is cut, summer begins. When summer vacation ends, autumn comes with all of its vibrant colors and cool fresh air. When autumn turns to winter, it is time for snuggling in warm blankets and drinking hot chocolate, and when winter ends — the hope of a new year begins again."

"Each season has a gift. Each ending brings a beginning. Can you remember the gifts of what was, and welcome the gifts of what is?"

Myra sat still, and silent, and allowed herself time to think about all that she had heard and felt.

She remembered the joy of being with her grandmothers again, and she smiled.

She touched her necklace and remembered the new way she was given to name and release all that had been too heavy to forget or forgive.

Then, in the space between saying "thank you" and "what's next," Myra jumped up like a cat does when startled by a bug or a shadow of themselves because suddenly, Christopher was again standing right beside her!

After they hugged and laughed a bit, Christopher continued,

"Let your grandmothers who love you dearly, and I who see you completely, be with you always. Talk to us. Let us listen and care for you and the love and loss that you are tempted to keep as a secret from yourself and others."

Then, Christopher leaned in closer and whispered,

"Myra, my ray, remember, you can always return to this island of love and letting go. But for now, you have done enough. Now you can rest."

Myra let Christopher's words sink into her heart and cried soft, easy tears like you do when someone is unexpectedly kind.

"Kindness always makes me cry," she whispered.

Myra's heart was opening and melting but her mind was still spinning like it does sometimes. So she looked down at her shoes, thrust her hands deep into her pockets and toyed with a loose thread.

"Can I trust what Christopher is telling me?" she asked herself while she paced in small circles.

"What if I haven't done enough? What if I forgot something, or didn't properly name every hurt or harm or mistake I have made?"

But, even before Myra had finished assembling her worries into neat rows of doubts, Christopher intervened with great and gentle authority.

"Yes, you have done enough. You are enough. And you are loved. As far as east is from west—that is how far removed you are from the weight of your worries."

With Christopher standing beside her, Myra looked up and saw the beautiful horizons stretched out before her with their infinitely varied tints, textures and contours.

She imagined what the bird's eye view of her would be from the perch of the oily-black raven on his crooked limb, and she straightened her back—making herself taller than she thought she had ever been.

She closed her eyes, pulled her head back and raised her arms up to the royal blue skies and felt, for a moment or two, that she too was in flight.

When Myra opened her eyes, she spotted a bright yellow airplane flying overhead—puffing and puttering and pulling a colorful block letter sign that read, "Finished. Over. Done."

Quite naturally, Myra bowed her head in prayers of gratitude and welcomed the sweet relief of love and loss and letting go. Her tears of both sadness and joy—rose tears, as some might call them—fell and watered the earth where she stood.

And after a time, Myra knew she was ready to move on.

CHAPTER 7

Myra Meets Carrot the Parrot

Myra walked with a lighter step back towards the island's shore, and with Christopher's help, stepped into the tiny boat again.

Yes, it was true. Myra was exceptionally happy but also — just plumb tired. So, she made herself a nest of lightly weighted blankets and fluffy soft pillows full of the smell of fresh air, and slept and slept while Christopher kept watch.

As Christopher guided the boat forward, he hummed a sweet little tune while making tea and snacks. He knew Myra would be ravishingly hungry when she woke up.

Several hours and nautical miles later, Myra opened her eyes to a steeping hot cup of her favorite black tea and a delightful plate of crackers and strawberry jam, and another surprise. A big, bold, green parrot perched at the end of the boat!

"Well, what is that parrot doing here?" exclaimed Myra. "And what is his name?"

"His name is Carrot," Christopher replied.

"Carrot?!" Myra yelled more loudly than she had intended. "Why in the world is he called Carrot when he is so very green?"

"Shouldn't he be called Grassy, or Lettuce, or Mossy, or some other thing that is the color he is?"

Carrot's little fluffy head drooped a bit as he tried to use his emerald green feathers to hide his pounding-too-fast heart.

You see, it wasn't the first time people had questioned his name — why he was named Carrot, something *so* orange, when he was *so obviously* green?

So it was indeed a surprise, and particularly welcomed, when Christopher spoke up so quickly and assuredly on Carrot's behalf.

"You see, Myra," Christopher kindly offered, "Carrot loves his name because he loves everything orange."

"Carrot loves the way orange smells—like when you peel a fresh tangerine in the morning for breakfast."

"Carrot loves the way orange looks—like the color of the sun in the beginning of day, and the big, bold harvest moon just on the edge of night."

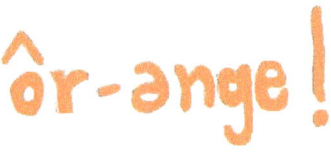

"But most of all," Christopher added, "Carrot loves the way orange *sounds*!

Why, can you think of any other word that rhymes with orange?"

Christopher watched as Myra looked up to her right, and then to her left — silently searching for a word to rhyme with orange.

When he saw Myra's initial enthusiasm turn from playful exploration to troubling frustration, he bent closer and whispered,

"You see, Myra, Carrot loves orange so much that no one has ever had the heart to tell him what he is not. Can you understand this kind of love?"

Myra thought carefully about all the things that Christopher had said. And then, she thought some more about what the parrot believed and what he loved.

"Yes," she finally replied.

"I DO understand how it feels to be called by a name that I love."

"I also understand," she added, "that sometimes it takes a little time for friends to see me as I see myself. But, I wonder, why is Carrot in MY boat?"

Christopher was glad when Myra asked this question because he always liked bringing good news. And this was the best yet!

"Carrot is here because he wants to be here — with you!" he exclaimed.

"You see, Carrot the Parrot is a volunteer, of sorts. He has offered to speak up for you and be your voice when you are afraid. Or help you find the right words to say how you are feeling, or ask for help when you need it. How does this sound to you?"

"That sounds very *orange*!" Myra exclaimed.

Smiling from ear to ear, Myra thanked the parrot for wanting to be in her boat and offered him a cracker, saying,

"Carrot, thank you for being who you are and for wanting to be with me as I am. And, thank you for being my companion. I believe we will be the best of friends for a very long time!"

CHAPTER 8

Who Do You Want in Your Boat?

Christopher loved seeing how happy both Myra and Carrot were in finding one another.

"You know, Myra, you always get to pick who you want to be in your boat with you. Who would you like to travel with you for the rest of this journey?"

Myra's eyes brightened as she gleefully answered, "That's easy! I would like a yellow puppy!"

Then, giggling like you do when you think about friends that you love, she enthusiastically added, "I would also like a white kitten to keep the puppy company. And a warm little house for them to snuggle in together when it gets rainy and cold."

And so, without much of ado at all, Myra found herself accompanied with her new and favorite friends.

While everyone was busy introducing themselves and getting settled in for their journey together, Myra noticed something moving in the front of the boat—just under the seat—in the dark corner not more than three feet away from her shoes.

"It's a SNAKE!" she screamed at the top of her lungs.

Myra stood up so quickly that the little boat nearly tipped over, and Carrot nearly fell from his most proper perch.

In a piercing high pitch, and with angry arms flailing, she looked directly at Christopher and accusingly yelled,

"I - DID - NOT invite a snake! How did you let THAT snake get into MY boat?"

"Myra," Christopher answered with his usual patience, "It is only one – little – tiny – snake. This snake is a part of nature just like you and me."

"I promise you," he went on, "as long as you keep track of where the snake is, he cannot sneak up on you. He cannot startle and scare you if you know who, and what, and where he is."

"Do you think you can practice this kind of trust and sit back down in the boat?"

And so, without much fuss or delay, Christopher, Myra, Carrot the Parrot, the puppy whom Myra named Puppy and the kitten named Kitty, and the snake whom Myra decided to call Shadow, settled in for the final leg of their journey home.

CHAPTER 9

Coming Home

A S they all found their favorite places in the boat for the final leg of their trip, the way westward was easy.

The winds were mostly at their backs and the waves were gentle. And everyone settled in nicely together—eating, sleeping, sipping tea, and visiting like you do when making new friends.

Myra was happy to share this time with her new friends, but she was also eager to get back to the familiar and simple joys of home. She laid her head back on a plaid blanket cushioning the wooden boat's rail, closed her eyes, and listened to the music of her friends talking, in the quietest of tones, beside her.

Myra soaked in the warmth of the sun on her face and let herself dream about sleeping in her own bed, doing ordinary things, eating ordinary foods, and—in what felt like no time at all—discovered that they had returned to the familiar rickety dock.

Myra gathered her things and reached for Christopher's hand as she stepped out of the boat. With his usual kindness he helped her step to the shore but—much to her surprise, and frankly dismay—he mistakenly called her Mary!

"Mary?" she quizzically asked herself. "How in this world can he possibly not remember my name after all that we have shared together?"

After taking her first wobbly steps back onto land, Myra found that she was not only confused by Christopher's mistake but also a little bit mad. She knew too that she could not keep her questions or feelings locked inside, and so she stated,

"Christopher, my name is Myra. How is it that you do not know my name by now? Is my name so easy to forget? Am *I* so easily forgotten now that our trip is over?"

Hearing her fear and disappointment, Christopher quickly assured her, "I have not forgotten your name, nor you."

Stopping where he was, and looking directly into her tearfully sad eyes, he went on to explain.

"I have always known you as Mary, which is not so different than Myra. After all, both names are spelled using the letters M-Y-R-A. The only difference is how the letters are re-arranged to spell M-A-R-Y."

Christopher looked to her for a sign that she was understanding and trusting him again, then added what he had longed to tell her since the start of their journey.

"You see, Myra, Mary is your forever name and the name of your soul."

"Well, I'll be!" Mary exclaimed as she plopped back down beside him and listened with renewed trust.

"Names are a funny and sacred thing," he said with what felt to Myra like a new kind of respect for her ability to believe in things bigger than herself.

"For example," he continued, "you first knew me as Christopher, but my father knows me as Christ which is my forever soul name. But some may choose to call me Chris — usually those who want to think of me less formally because of being scared by bigger people who were at one time not so kind to them."

Watching for the degree of Myra's understanding and desire to know more, Christopher went on.

"I have other names and nicknames," he added. "But ultimately I answer to whatever name is used with love to call me close."

They sat like that together in comfortable silence for quite a while—like friends do when thinking about tender and meaningful things. And, after a time, Christopher added one last offering.

"So, you see, dear one, I know all of my names. I know who I am, and now you know who you are too."

Mary listened, and nodded, and agreed that this was indeed good and true. Then, gathering Carrot, Puppy, Kitty, and Shadow too, they all walked home, together.

THE BEGINNING

Conversation Starters

The story of Myra's journey to the Island of Letting Go is written with a desire to meet you where you are—in the mood for whimsy, or open to a deeper experience in healing a tender heart. Or both!

The text and illustrations are presented, hopefully, with enough detail to portray the spirit of the story while also leaving room for imagination and discovery of your own story, words and images.

Contact us if you are interested in receiving additional information about conversation starters including more background about some of the characters and questions you may wish to ponder in your personal quiet time or in community with others.

May you dare to step into
bold reckonings with your past,
and even bolder dreams for your future.

www.sacredsupport.com

Thank You

No words will ever come close to saying how grateful I am for my two grandmothers—for when I was growing up on the farm, and here in the city in my meditation. Sensing their loving presence again was such a surprise and delight that night seven years ago. I still feel rose tears today as I prepare to share their love with and for you.

It's a dicey business, this naming of specific individuals who showed up as sunshine and rain on the seeds of a story. I take the risk because not doing it would mean missing out on the fun of sharing names of those who helped support me along the way.

To start out, thank you Carrie Hirdes. Little did we know that our questions and discernments in 2014 would be answered and delivered as promised. Thank you also for your enthusiasm as my first writing coach. You opened my eyes to finding what works and gently dismissing what does not, and the joy of sharing and supporting fellow writers as sisters and brothers, not competitors.

Thank you also to one of the first readers of the story, Mary Fuller. Your early encouragement, and frankly, your finding a place in your heart for Carrot was a green light to my soul to keep going.

I'm grateful to Kathryn Lanning Herman for the photos of her beloved parrot, Chico. They were sweet references for illustrating Carrot on the pages. And, thank you to my friends, especially my fellow author and buddy Barb, who in response to me crying that I couldn't do the art well enough said, "You can do this, Treese."

Thank you, Larisa Fai-Yengo, for remembering the moment and the mood on the night when the story of Carrot first showed up; and thank you to all of the others who sat with me in silent companionship, then and now and every Tuesday night, as we seek connections with Love.

And to Les, my dear husband, friend and editor, you are my forever companion and champion. Thank you for once again enduring my meltdowns, tears, and curses, as well as for sharing your extraordinary gift for grammar. I'm so very grateful we share this passion for the creative work process that includes trying to make it the best that we can—even when that is not perfect. I love you dearly.

About the Author

Theresa was born in a small farming town in Illinois. She is an author, artist, spiritual director/companion, wife, friend, and fellow journeyer.

Trained through the Pecos Benedictine School of Spiritual Direction, Theresa draws from her life within Christianity as well as embracing the teachings of Zen Buddhism and philosophy. She shares and does not skirt the spiritual disciplines she has found necessary to continue living the practical business of recovery, surviving loss, and moving through the natural passages of aging, and embraces the challenges and grace of a loving God.

Theresa continues to write, walks with others as spiritual director, is an active participant in her own recovery, and celebrates life and travel with her husband.

SACRED SUPPORT PUBLISHING llc
A Place for Good Words & Good Works

Sacred Support Publishing, LLC was established for the purpose of encouraging and supporting artists and indie authors. Other offerings from Sacred Support Publishing:

ROSETEARS:
A Journey of Loving God, Loving Ourselves, and Loving Others

The ROSETEARS Discovery Journal:
A Workbook Companion to Rosetears

The St. Francis Prayer Discovery Journal:
12 Prayers for Personal Peace

Friday Love Notes for the Soul:
52 Meditations in Just a Few Words
and a Little Bit of Art

Please contact us for information about special pricing on group orders, Conversation Starters and/or support for book studies, and for contributions from writers and authors, artists and other encouragers of the soul. We hope you will find this sacred space to be a place for good words and good works.

Sacred Support Publishing llc
Houston, Texas
www.sacredsupport.com

141